D0481292

7/96

A Sound
of Leaves

Other books by *Lenore* and *Erik Blegvad*

Anna Banana and Me

Rainy Day Kate

Other books by *Lenore Blegvad*

Once Upon a Time and Grandma

Other books illustrated by *Erik Blegvad*

*With One White Wing: Puzzles in
Poems and Pictures,* by Elizabeth Spires

Twelve Tales, by Hans Christian Andersen

Water Pennies and Other Poems, by N. M. Bodecker

(MARGARET K. MCELDERRY BOOKS)

Lenore Blegvad

A Sound of Leaves

*Illustrated
by
Erik Blegvad*

MARGARET K. MCELDERRY BOOKS

To friends and friendship,
everywhere
—L. B. & E. B.

Margaret K. McElderry Books
An imprint of Simon & Schuster Children's Publishing Division
1230 Avenue of the Americas
New York, New York 10020

Text copyright © 1996 by Lenore Blegvad
Illustrations copyright © 1996 by Erik Blegvad

Book design by Michael Nelson
The text of this book is set in Berkeley Old Style.
The illustrations were rendered in pencil

Printed in the United States of America
1 3 5 7 9 10 8 6 4 2

Library of Congress Cataloging-in-Publication Data
Blegvad, Lenore.
A sound of leaves / Lenore Blegvad ;
illustrated by Erik Blegvad.
p. cm.
Summary: Nine-year-old Sylvie and her family
leave the city for a week at a beach house
where everything feels different.
ISBN 0-689-80038-X
[1. Beaches—Fiction. 2. Vacations—Fiction.
3. Homesickness—Fiction. 4. Family life—Fiction.]
I. Blegvad, Erik, ill. II. Title.
PZ7.B618So 1995
[Fic]—dc20
94-46961
CIP
AC

Contents

I

The Tree

*I*t wasn't a pretty house. But perhaps it would be all right. They couldn't be sure looking at it. It was Mom's cousin's house. But even so, it was strange to them because they had never seen it before.

Nor had they seen this street full of wooden houses nor this town they had come to.

They knew no one there at all.

And strange too was the sight of pale sand under their feet, blown in from the nearby beach.

The taxi that had brought them from the station drove off and left them—Grandpa, Sylvie, Mom, and Dell.

Sylvie, who was nine, stared at the low house, at the screened porch, at the peeling wooden steps.

Her brother, Dell, who was six, stared down the road after the departing taxi.

"There's grass," Sylvie said, moving toward the patch of it in front of the porch.

"There's supposed to be a backyard," said Mom, peering along the brown side of the house.

One by one they bumped their duffel bags up the steps onto the porch. Mom had a key to the front door.

Sylvie went inside first. She saw a big room with scuff-marked walls, sunlight on floorboards, wooden chairs around a table. There was a couch but not

much else. A few magazines lay scattered here and
there. And under the low ceiling it was hot.

Beyond, she could see two bedrooms. In the
smaller one the afternoon sun made a green-
ish light. It shone in through a thick layer of
leaves pressing against the screen of one of the
two windows.

"That little room can be yours, if you want,"
said Mom.

"Yes, please," Sylvie said, and going into it she
gazed through the glass at the greenery. It looked as
if the branches and leaves would reach right into
the room if the window were open. There were so
many, maybe they would fill up the whole room.

Holding her breath, Sylvie thought about that. Then, putting her duffel bag down on the narrow bed, she tried to open the window. It did not budge. The window frame was splintered here and there and flakes of paint were peeling from it. Later, she could ask Grandpa to help her with it.

Sylvie smiled. "I have a tree," she whispered to herself.

2

A Lot to Learn

"What a mess," Mom said.

They had finished unpacking and were standing in the backyard on the only bit of grass left between the overgrown bushes.

"It's creepy out here," Dell said. "Like in a jungle."

Above them the trees blocked out almost all the sunlight. A bird chirped in the tallest one.

Sylvie pushed her way quickly through the bushes to the tree growing outside her window. She put her cheek against its cool trunk.

"He said we could cut some bushes back," Grandpa was saying to Mom.

In a shed stood a weather-beaten table and some plastic chairs. There was a rolled-up hammock, a rusty lawn mower, a few tools.

"We'll sure have to do something," said Mom. "We can't even sit down."

She had talked a lot about sitting in her own backyard for a week. Almost as much as about living next to a beach.

"Does this tree have a name?" Sylvie asked.

The others all turned to look at it.

"What about Herman?" suggested Grandpa.

"Oh, Grandpa!" Sylvie giggled. "I mean what kind is it?"

Mom came and looked up and down its trunk.

"Good question," she said. "What do we know about trees? Nothing. But we're learning, we're learning."

Dell said, "I want to go to the beach. This is too creepy."

"Oh, can we, Mom?" Sylvie cried.

"Tomorrow," said Mom, taking Dell's hand. "It's getting late. We still have to make our beds. Grandpa's tired and I'm hungry. Tomorrow we'll go. We'll have a picnic. Agreed?"

They agreed, imagining how perfect that would be, even if they had never done such a thing before.

3

Listening

Mom turned on the two dim lamps in the living room. She moved one closer to the table where they had begun to eat the food they had brought from the city.

Dell chewed on a carrot and looked around the room, at the lumpy sofa where Mom said she was going to sleep.

"I don't know if I like it here," he announced glumly.

Sylvie stopped eating to watch him. She didn't want him to be unhappy. She saw him squirm on his wooden chair and squint out the window

beyond Grandpa, where there was another unfamiliar house, not far away.

Grandpa spread mustard carefully on a slice of salami.

"When you come to a decision," he said to Dell, "be sure and tell us, okay?"

Sylvie hoped his teasing wouldn't make Dell cry. But Grandpa winked at Dell.

Mom sighed. "I'll tell *you* something first," she said to Dell. "You don't know anything yet, so you can't say you don't like it. And no matter what, we're here for a week."

Sylvie saw Dell's lower lip push out.

Mom reached out to pat one of Dell's thin arms. "Anyway," she said, "we're all here together. It'll be fine. There's the beach. There's the yard. It's the country! You'll see, you'll love it!"

Dell's frown only deepened. "We're not together," he said. "Dad's not here."

"Well, I told you," Mom said. "You know he can't come. You know he has to work. And he has to work this weekend too. I *told* you. And we decided to come, remember?"

Dell sniffed and took another bite of his carrot.

Sylvie missed Dad too. She and Dell had never been anywhere where Dad wasn't. Come to think of it, they had never been anywhere much at all. To Grandpa's apartment before Grandma had died. That was all. Now Grandpa lived with them.

They had never ever been to the country.

Sylvie missed Dad, and what's more, she needed him. Her window was stuck. Even Grandpa couldn't open it.

Dad could have done it in a minute. He could fix things. He worked in a garage back in the city. And if Dad were here, maybe it wouldn't feel so strange.

The strangeness hung on Sylvie's shoulders, like a heavy coat.

The house felt strange, even though it belonged to Mom's cousin. He had lent it to them for a week and had sent them the key. But they did not know him, she and Dell.

So there was a strangeness.

To the rooms and to the chairs and tables.

To the fingerprints on the refrigerator door.

To the places where knives and forks were kept.

To the shapes of knobs and faucets. To the country silence outside in the dark road; such a loud silence that Sylvie had to say, "Listen!"

They all stopped eating.

"To what?" asked Dell.

"To nothing!" said Sylvie. "To no cars! To no sirens!"

"You're right," said Mom. "To no kids hollering in the street!"

"And no feet galumphing down stairways!" said Grandpa.

"And no loud music from next door!" said Dell, who hated that at home.

"And maybe there won't be noisy garbage trucks at night!" Sylvie added.

Then in the silence they began to hear something after all. A faint chirruping sound, then many many more, one sound on top of the other.

"Chir-rup, chir-rup, chir-rup."

"What's that?" Sylvie asked.

"It's crickets!" Grandpa said. "That's what you hear at night in the country. Crickets!"

And listening, Sylvie heard something else as

well. The gentle sound of leaves brushing against the screen outside her window: *woosh-woosh-woosh.*

That was a strangeness, too, but to Sylvie, a private and happy one.

4

The Tide Comes In

Sylvie walked carefully over the rippled patterns in the sand, through shallow pools of sea-green water, out toward the horizon. Tiptoeing, she made her way between dark little shells half-buried in the wet sand.

The tide was low. Sand and shallow water spread before her until they met the sky. Behind her, a long way off, lay the beach. Overhead a sea gull followed her as she went, its cry filling the pale sky. "Kree-aw! Kree-aw!"

She wanted to call back to it. *Well*, she could, couldn't she. Why not? No one could hear her. She

gave a cry like the gull's and it cried back at her. "Kree-aw!"

Far away on the beach a tiny Mom waved to her. A tiny Dell was digging in the sand. Next to him she could see Grandpa, eating the last of their picnic lunch. All of them were wearing baseball hats from the garage where Dad worked. Sylvie waved her hat at Mom as she wandered on.

Soon she came to a flat rock poking up out of the sandy shallows. It was perfect for standing on and for hopping on and off. But before long the water began to lap over her toes, and all around her the rippled sand was disappearing. Sylvie remembered hearing about tides at school. The tide had turned. It was time to go. With splashing steps, she returned to the beach.

Only a few people were left on it. Some children who had been sitting near them picked up their towels.

"They look like nice kids," Mom said.

"Better brush off the sand," Grandpa advised as they put on their sneakers. "You'll hate it in your bed tonight."

Sylvie would not hate anything about today. Sun and sand and sea gulls were inside her head forever.

But now the air was turning cool. Their dry shirts were warm over their damp bathing suits.

"Hey, I'm salty," Dell said delightedly, licking his arm.

And so were all of them. Wonderfully, wonderfully salty.

To get home, they had to climb over the seawall bordering the road, a wall of big boulders.

"Watch your step," Mom told them.

Grandpa carried the plastic bag with the picnic garbage and their wet towels. Mom carried the empty apple juice bottle in one hand and helped Dell over the rocks with the other.

Sylvie stepped carefully from one rock to another. Above her Dell stumbled along, helped by Mom.

But all at once Sylvie saw Dell slip and begin to

fall, saw Mom pull on his hand to steady him, saw Mom lose her balance as well.

Down they tumbled, Dell and Mom, in between the rocks! The apple juice bottle crashed and shattered into a million pieces.

Dell was all right. He only had a skinned elbow.

But Mom! Mom fell onto a piece of glass and cut her leg badly. Blood ran down onto her sneaker.

"Oh, Mama!" Sylvie called out.

Dell began to cry. Grandpa took off his shirt and wrapped it tightly around Mom's leg.

Mom sat, pale and silent, where she had fallen. Sylvie and Dell huddled next to her.

"Stay right there," Grandpa said to them. "I'm going up to the road to stop a car."

19

He came back with a young man and together they helped Mom up to the car. Sylvie and Dell scrambled up after them.

"He says he can take us to a doctor," Grandpa said to Sylvie. "But his car is so small, we'll have to squeeze to get in."

It was a *very* small car. Sylvie could see that. They would have to sit on top of each other.

Suddenly she said, "I could take Dell home! It's just around that corner. I can take him home!"

Grandpa frowned and looked at Mom.

She sat in the car pressing Grandpa's shirt tightly to her leg.

"All right," Mom said. "She can do that."

"Do you remember where we put the key?" Grandpa asked.

Sylvie nodded and reached for Dell's hand. But just before the car started up, she ran to the window. "Mama," she cried out again. "Are you going to be all right?"

Inside the car Mom nodded, sharply and quickly, many little nods. Nod, nod, nod.

"Yes," she said in a fierce whisper. "It's only a cut. Don't worry. Now go home."

And the car drove off.

Sylvie took Dell's hand again. "Come on," she said.

Almost pulling him along the road, she only partly noticed houses and lawns and yards and porches as they went. Nor did she notice that the sea had by now almost covered all of the rippled sand.

Turning the corner of their road she did notice a big house set back on a wide green lawn. A striped awning extended beyond a glassed-in porch.

She thought she saw one of the children from the beach, a girl, running over the lawn.

Sylvie knew Dell was going to cry soon. He was too silent, trotting along beside her. Sure enough, as she opened their door with the key she took from under a stone in the yard, he began to howl. Sylvie shut the door and put her arms around him, just like Mom would have done, and Dell stopped crying. Side by side, they sat on the couch, waiting to see what would happen.

Was Mom going to be all right? Would they have to go home? Sylvie wondered. Would that be the end of the beach, the end of their week in the country?

Dad would be in the city. And Lucia, her best friend who lived downstairs. But oh, how Sylvie hoped they could stay at the beach.

Sitting on the couch, she could hear the branches outside her window scraping lightly on the screen. It was a comforting sound. Somehow she was sure that if she could only open the window and let the branches in, everything would be better.

5

Fresh Sights

The next morning Grandpa cut back some of the bushes in the yard. When there was enough space, he tied up the hammock between two trees. Then he took Dell to the beach.

Mom lay in the hammock with her eyes closed.

Sylvie sat beside her on the grass eating one of the jelly sandwiches that, all by herself, she had made everyone for lunch. She and Dell were going to take turns keeping Mom company.

Mom's sandwich still lay on a paper napkin, balancing on her stomach.

"Not right now," she had said, when Sylvie had brought it out to her.

Taped to Mom's leg was a big bandage. It covered the stitches the doctor had put in.

"You may have sprained your ankle as well," he had said. "Better stay off it. No swimming, no beach, no sand."

So Mom lay in the hammock with her eyes closed.

Inside the house the phone rang. Sylvie ran in to answer it.

"How's Mom?" Dad's voice asked. He was on his lunch break in the city. "Does she want to come home?"

"I don't know," Sylvie told him. "I guess she's thinking about it right now."

After a while Mom opened her eyes.

"Are we going home?" Sylvie asked her at once.

Mom looked up at the leaves over her head. Sylvie held her breath.

"We should," Mom said. "If we don't, it will be a lot of trouble for you and Grandpa with me just lying here. A big team effort."

"That's okay," Sylvie said quickly. "We can do it."

Mom nodded. "Well, maybe." She closed her eyes again.

Sylvie lay back on the grass. From under one hand she slowly pulled up a single blade of grass and chewed on its bitter pale end.

"I should have known," she heard Mom say. "I should have known. But that's life, I guess." Raising her head, Mom tried to look at the bandage on her leg.

The hammock began to sway.

"Ooh," she cried. "This thing makes me dizzy!"

Sylvie sat up and steadied the hammock with her hand.

Mom began to eat her sandwich.

"M-m-m-m good," she said. "Did you make it? And for everybody?"

Sylvie nodded. She lay back again on the grass. Turning her head she could see into the clearing Grandpa had made. There the grass was a darker green, and beyond was a border of growing things—ferns and a bed of flattened stalks. A white stone glittered in a splash of sunlight. Under the border a beetle worked its way up and down over the bumpy earth. Above a spiderweb stretched, trembling, between stems of yellow flowers.

Sylvie did not know which thing to look at first.

And there was so much more!

"It's pretty here, isn't it?" Mom asked.

"Then can we stay?" Sylvie asked again.

Mom smiled a kind of sad smile. "Okay," she said. "Why not? We'll manage. But it isn't how I meant it to be."

Sylvie knew it wasn't.

Picnics on the beach, going fishing, picking flowers—that was what Mom had meant it to be. But it didn't matter. There were beetles and ferns to look at. There was still lots for them to do together.

Just then two sea gulls came swooping overhead. Squawking, they chased each other toward the beach.

Sylvie looked up. "Kree-aw!" she called after them.
Mom laughed at the sound. The hammock began
to sway. "Oh, drat this thing!" Mom cried out.
But it was going to be all right.

6

Along the Way

"Do they have sprinkles?" Dell asked.

They did.

And holding his ice-cream cone in both hands, he slowly followed Sylvie home, as if in a dream.

The ice-cream stand was in the next street to theirs, outside the grocery.

Walking home they came first to the beach and passed along in front of the dark horizon of the sea. It was a gray day. The waves foamed heavily onto the empty beach.

When they came to the big lawn on their corner, Sylvie saw one of the girls she had seen at the beach. She was sitting on the grass near the road, leaning against a tree, eating an apple.

"Hi," the girl said. She had straight blond hair. She was older than Sylvie.

"Hello," Sylvie said, stopping in the road.

Dell went on walking in his dream.

"What kind did you get?" the girl asked.

That stopped Dell. "Fudge ripple!" he announced. "With sprinkles!"

Both girls laughed at his chocolate-smeared face.

"He your brother?" the blond girl asked.

Sylvie nodded.

"I saw you on the beach the other day," the girl said. "But I haven't seen you since."

Sylvie licked her cone. Butterscotch, not fudge ripple. "I'm taking care of my mom. She's got a cut on her leg. With stitches."

"Come on, Sylvie," Dell said.

Sylvie remained where she was. "Go on," she told him. "It's just a few houses more. I'll be there in a minute."

But Dell stood waiting.

The girl looked up at the clouds. "It's going to

rain," she said. "That's why the others aren't coming, I guess."

Sylvie glanced down the road. No "others" were in sight. A drop of rain fell on her cheek. As she too looked up at the sky, she noticed the leaves on the tree over the girl's head. Weren't they the same as those on her very own tree?

"Do you know about trees?" she asked the girl.

"Trees? You mean what kind they are?"

Sylvie nodded.

"No," the girl said. "Not really." She took a bite of her apple. "But I've got a book about them," she added when she had finished chewing.

More raindrops fell. The girl got up. "I'll show it to you if you want. But you better come tomorrow. After lunch. Got to go in now."

"Sylvie!" Dell called then. "It's sprinkling on my sprinkles!"

The girl laughed.

"So long, Sylvie," she said. "And my name's Clair," she added. Then off she ran over the green lawn.

Big drops splashed on the tar road. Sylvie and

Dell ran toward their house. And running in the rain, Sylvie was happy. Tomorrow I'll find out about my tree, she thought. And I'll see Clair again. She had never had a country friend before.

7

Hidden Places

*A*ll the leaves look the same," Sylvie said the next day.

She turned the pages in Clair's tree book, trying to find one like those on her tree.

"They don't really," said Clair. "Some have more points than others. Some have smooth edges, see?"

On Clair's awninged porch it was shady and cool. Pretty glass tables stood in front of bamboo chairs filled with plump cushions. On one table lay a plate of cookies. A lady had brought them out. Not Clair's mother, who was away on a trip somewhere. On another table a silver vase held a bouquet of pale flowers. In the next room a grand-father clock ticked the seconds calmly.

"I'm looking for the name of a special tree. But I can't tell which one it is from these pictures," Sylvie said. "I think it's like the one you were sitting under yesterday."

Clair looked up from the book. "Oh that! Why didn't you say so? That's a dogwood. It has big white flowers in the spring. See, here it is."

She turned back a few pages.

Dogwood. That was a nice name. And big white flowers in the spring. Sylvie liked that. "There's one in our yard," she explained. "It's going to come into my room, through the window."

"It is?" Clair sounded confused. "Well anyway, that's neat. Trees are nice." She leaned back into the cushions.

So are you, Sylvie thought, smiling at her new friend. She was about to explain further when someone shouted from outside.

"Hey, Clair! Are you ready?"

Clair jumped up to look out of the big windows.

"Come on," she said to Sylvie. "The others are here. We're going to the beach. I forgot. Want to come?"

Sylvie looked too. The others were the children she had first seen with Clair. Two big boys. Another girl. Sylvie shook her head.

"I can't go to the beach without my grandpa. And I have to go home soon anyway."

The others came trooping up onto the sunporch with a noisy stomping of their white sneakers and a jingling of the silver charm bracelet the girl wore on one sunburned arm. Seeing Sylvie, they fell silent, staring. They stared at her, at the tree book, at the plate of cookies on the table.

Sylvie looked down at her feet. There was a hole in one of her sneakers.

"This is Sylvie," Clair said.

"Hi." The response was brief.

Then, with a glance toward the cookies, the girl said, "Can we have one of those?"

Clair nodded.

In a flash, the cookies were gone.

"What are you two doing in here?" one boy asked then.

"Reading my tree book," Clair told him.

Wrinkling his nose the boy looked from Clair to Sylvie and back again. "Terrific," he commented

The other boy turned to the door. "You coming with us, Clair?" he asked.

Clair hesitated.

"Sylvie can't go," she said. "What if we play something first and go later? Like hide-and-seek?"

"That'll take too long," one grumbled. "I've got a piano lesson."

"Just one game?" Clair said.

"We have to be home early," the other two complained. "It won't leave much time."

But finally they agreed.

What they wanted to do was go to the beach. With Clair. Sylvie could tell that easily. They didn't want to play hide-and-seek or *anything* with her. And they didn't like her. She was sure of that too.

"I better go home now," she said, edging toward the glass door of the porch.

Clair took her arm. "Oh, come on," she said. "We'll just play one game."

One of the boys was "it." He began counting to one hundred at a furious pace. The others ran off over the lawn.

All except Sylvie. Where could she possibly
hide in this unknown place? In a panic she turned
around and around; looking, looking. Then, nearby, she saw a tiny opening underneath some
dense bushes. She was just barely small enough
to slip into it.

Prickly leaves scratched her arms and legs. The
earth she had to curl up on was cold and damp, and
her heart was thumping wildly. It was horrible
under there and clear that no one had ever hidden
there before.

"I should have gone home," she whispered to
herself, over and over. "I should have gone home."
But she hadn't. It would have spoiled everything.
It would have been like losing her new friend just
after finding her.

Soon Sylvie heard whoops and shrieks and running feet. The others had been found.

"But you haven't found Sylvie," Clair's voice
said, laughing.

"I will in a minute," one boy said. "Here, Sylvie,
Sylvie. Where are you, Sylvie, Sylvie?" His feet
stamped over the lawn. The others followed

him here and there to the jingling of the charm bracelet. Their voices faded away again.

Now was Sylvie's chance to run out, to touch the tree, to be "Home Free"! But it was already too late. She could hear them coming back.

And this time they sounded angry.

"I don't care if we never find her," the other girl was saying. "Let's stop. I want to go to the beach."

"Yeah, who cares?" one boy said.

"Okay, I give up," said the other. "And who is she anyway, this Sylvie? Where'd she come from, all of a sudden like that?"

"I can guess," the other girl said. "You just have to look at her. She's probably some little slum kid from the city. Who cares? Come on, Clair. We're going. You coming, or are you going to wait for her forever?"

Clair did not reply right away.

Under the bushes, Sylvie covered her ears as tightly as she could. But it didn't help. She could still hear the answer when it came.

"Okay," Clair said. "Let's go."

8

Taking Turns

"Who do they think they are?" said Grandpa angrily. "Little slum kid! I like that!"

"What do they know?" Mom said. "Nothing!" She gave one of her sighs. "They're just kids. It's what they learn at home. That's life."

Mom and Sylvie lay together in the hammock, their arms around each other. The hammock was almost touching the ground under their weight.

Sylvie could still feel the scratches from the prickly bushes. I'll feel them forever, she thought. But she had stopped crying now.

Running from Clair's, stumbling across the big

lawn and down the sandy street, she had not cried. Not until she had reached home and her own backyard where Mom lay reading in the hammock and Grandpa was oiling the lawn mower and Dell was pushing his toy cars in the shade under her very own dogwood tree. She had cried then.

Now Mom smoothed Sylvie's hair back with slow, firm strokes. "That's life," she said again. "They just don't know any better."

Sylvie closed her eyes. Aloud she said, "How come they didn't like me? They didn't even know me."

Dell, lying on his stomach, banged one toy car into another.

"Well, I sure don't like *them*," he said gloomily.

"Don't be silly," Grandpa scolded. "That's exactly what we're talking about. You don't know them at all."

"I don't have to," Dell said. "But they just might want to beat me up, like in the city. So I don't like them."

Lying there, Sylvie thought about that. She could tell Dell was *afraid* of the kids. He said he didn't like

them, but he was *afraid*. That's what it really was.

But that wasn't what had happened at Clair's, was it? Then what had?

"I didn't do anything," Sylvie said, thinking out loud. "I was just looking at a book, with Clair. They wanted to go to the beach."

"So do I!" said Dell, jumping up. "Grandpa, can't we go to the beach now?"

"It's Sylvie's turn," Mom reminded him. "It's your turn to stay with me. We're going to have cupcakes out here in the yard, remember?"

In the hammock Sylvie pressed a little closer to Mom. Those kids might still be at the beach! How could she go there? How could she ever go to the beach again?

But then what about her favorite rock? And the sea gulls she could hear calling? And what about the tide that would be turning soon? And the days that were rushing by?

Finally she made up her mind. She slipped carefully from the tippy hammock.

"Grandpa," she said. "Do you think we could sit in another place today?"

"You bet," Grandpa said. "But those kids don't own the beach, you know."

Sylvie hesitated. "Is it like giving in if I sit somewhere else?"

"No," Mom said in a firm voice. "Not today, it isn't. It's a good idea. It'll give you time to figure things out."

Sylvie knew there were things to figure out. But it was hard to know what they were, or where to begin.

With Splashing Steps

The beach was almost empty. The other children had already left. Grandpa said he'd like to spank the bunch of them if he saw them.

Sylvie, sitting next to him, pushed a hollow in the sand with her heels.

"They'd really like me then," she said glumly.

"Guess you're right," Grandpa said. He lay back on his neatly arranged towel.

Sylvie squinted at the bright sky above the horizon. The sun twinkled and sparkled on the shallow pools along the beach. Two white sailboats followed each other far out on the shining water.

Watching them, Sylvie poured a few fistfuls of sand onto her bare toes. Then, with a sigh, she lay back next to Grandpa, using her sneakers as a pillow.

Grandpa turned to look at her.

"You okay?" he asked.

"I guess so," Sylvie said. "But I can't help thinking about Clair."

"I know," Grandpa said.

Side by side, drowsy under the comforting heat of the sun, they lay listening to the gulls.

After a while, Grandpa sat up. "If you're going into the water," he said, "you should go now. It's getting late."

"Okay," Sylvie said, getting to her feet. She put on her baseball cap. "Is it all right if I go out to my rock?"

Grandpa said it was.

How good the warm shallow water felt on her feet.

Stamping through it was even nicer. And kicking up big splashes as she went was best of all. *Splash! Splash! Splash!*

By the time she reached her rock, Sylvie was feeling better. Stepping up on it she stood facing out to sea. Overhead a few sea gulls coasted silently on the light breeze.

All around the rock, under the water, lay a scattering of brown snail shells. Tiny pink seashells drifted this way and that in the wavelets.

"I'm going to take some seashells home to Mom," Sylvie said to herself. She gathered a few and looked at them as they lay in her palm. Almost transparent, a pale and delicate pink, they were the prettiest things she had ever seen.

"I'll take some home for Lucia too," she decided and gathered some more, putting them in her baseball cap. Thinking about Lucia reminded her of the city. What a lot she would have to tell her friend when she got home! Good things. And bad.

Lucia had never been to the country. Just like Sylvie. They were city girls, both of them. That's what they were.

"Just two little slum kids from the city," Sylvie said to herself. It almost made her laugh out loud.

Well, I bet living in a city is something these kids don't know anything about, she thought. If one of them showed up there, she and Lucia could teach them a thing or two, could show them how it feels to look wrong, talk wrong, to be left out. She and Lucia were a team and they would *never* let any of those kids in.

Stooping, Sylvie reached to pluck another shell from the water, one half-buried in the sand. Pale gold instead of pink, it made her think of Clair's blond hair.

But suppose, just suppose, Clair actually did come one day to the city. Suppose it was Clair sitting on the end of Sylvie's bed, looking down through the fire escape at the kids in the street below. Sitting where Lucia always sat. And what if Lucia came in then? Sylvie could just imagine her frown and how her cheeks would turn red like they always did when she got angry. She'd probably say, "Where'd *she* spring from?" or something else Sylvie would wish she hadn't. It would be awful.

Turning, Sylvie looked toward the faraway beach where Grandpa sat. He waved and she waved gratefully back at him. Looking around her, she saw the

sea was beginning to wash over her rock. It was time to go home. Clutching her baseball cap full of shells to her chest, Sylvie headed for the beach.

And then she saw Clair.

Clair was stooping in the shallow water closer to the beach, picking things up and putting them into a plastic pail. She was alone.

Sylvie stopped where she was. Her feet seemed to sink into the sand beneath the water. She hadn't planned on meeting Clair so soon, and in a minute Clair would see her. There was no hiding place out here. What should she do?

The air felt chilly then. Sylvie shivered as she watched Clair moving slowly through the water, the sun gleaming on her pale hair.

And at that very same moment, Sylvie understood what had happened at Clair's house.

"She had to choose," she whispered to herself. "That's what it was. She had to choose between those kids and me. Like I might have to choose between her and Lucia one day."

But now, instead of feeling chilled, she felt hot anger, and with one foot she gave a great kick that sent a huge splash of water high, high, up into the air! Back it fell in a sparkling shower of droplets, pattering onto her hair, her back, and the water around her.

"Crazy!" Sylvie almost shouted out loud. "That's the craziest thing I ever heard of."

Why should she have to choose? Couldn't they get along, *all* of them, if they really tried? Couldn't *everybody*, if they really wanted to?

And taking a deep breath, she began splashing noisily toward Clair.

Clair heard her. She stood up and saw Sylvie coming. Sylvie could read surprise and something like shyness on Clair's face.

"Hi!" Sylvie called out to her. "What are those things you're putting into your pail?"

"Jingle shells," Clair answered. "I'm going to make them into a necklace."

"Are they shells like mine?" Sylvie asked. Moving closer to Clair, she held out her baseball cap. Clair peered into it.

"Yes," Clair said. "That's what I've got."

They looked at each other for a long moment.

Sylvie took another deep breath.

"Will you show me how to make a necklace?" she asked.

Just for a second Clair hesitated. Then she smiled, a slow friendly smile that lit up her whole face.

"Sure," she said. "We need to find some more, though. And then I'll show you how, up at my house."

10

Hurry, Hurry!

*A*fter supper Sylvie sat on her bed and looked at her seashell necklace. She had proudly worn it in the backyard when she had come home from Clair's.

"Hey, that's neat!" Dell had said.

"Beautiful!" said Grandpa.

"Better than diamonds!" Mom said. "Good for you!"

Now the necklace hung from a point of splintered wood sticking out of her window frame. How pretty the pink shells looked next to the green leaves beyond the screen.

And tomorrow Clair was coming! For cupcakes in the yard!

Sylvie stared happily at her necklace. Then, looking to see if it was hanging firmly by its string, she noticed something. The little splinter of wood was really the head of a little nail. And on the other side of the window frame she saw another. They could hardly be seen in the peeling paint.

Sylvie caught her breath. The other window in her room had no little nails. Could they be the reason this window didn't open?

"Grandpa!" Sylvie called, running to get him. "Come and see! I think my window is nailed shut! We didn't see them! Tiny little nails!"

Grandpa fetched some tools from the shed in the backyard.

"You have sharp eyes, I must say. I never saw those."

He felt the little nails with his finger. Then he pulled them out, one by one. And slowly, carefully, he checked the frame for others.

Sylvie could hardly keep still. "Hurry, Grandpa! Hurry!" she cried.

Dell came in from the living room to watch. Mom called from the sofa, "Move over, Dell. I can't see from here." Because Grandpa, with Sylvie helping, was pushing open the window. Then he was unhooking the screen.

And then, with a snapping and swooshing, the branches of the dogwood tree sprang into Sylvie's room! Just as she had known they would!

They didn't fill the whole room, but Sylvie could tell that from her bed, she would be able to touch the leaves.